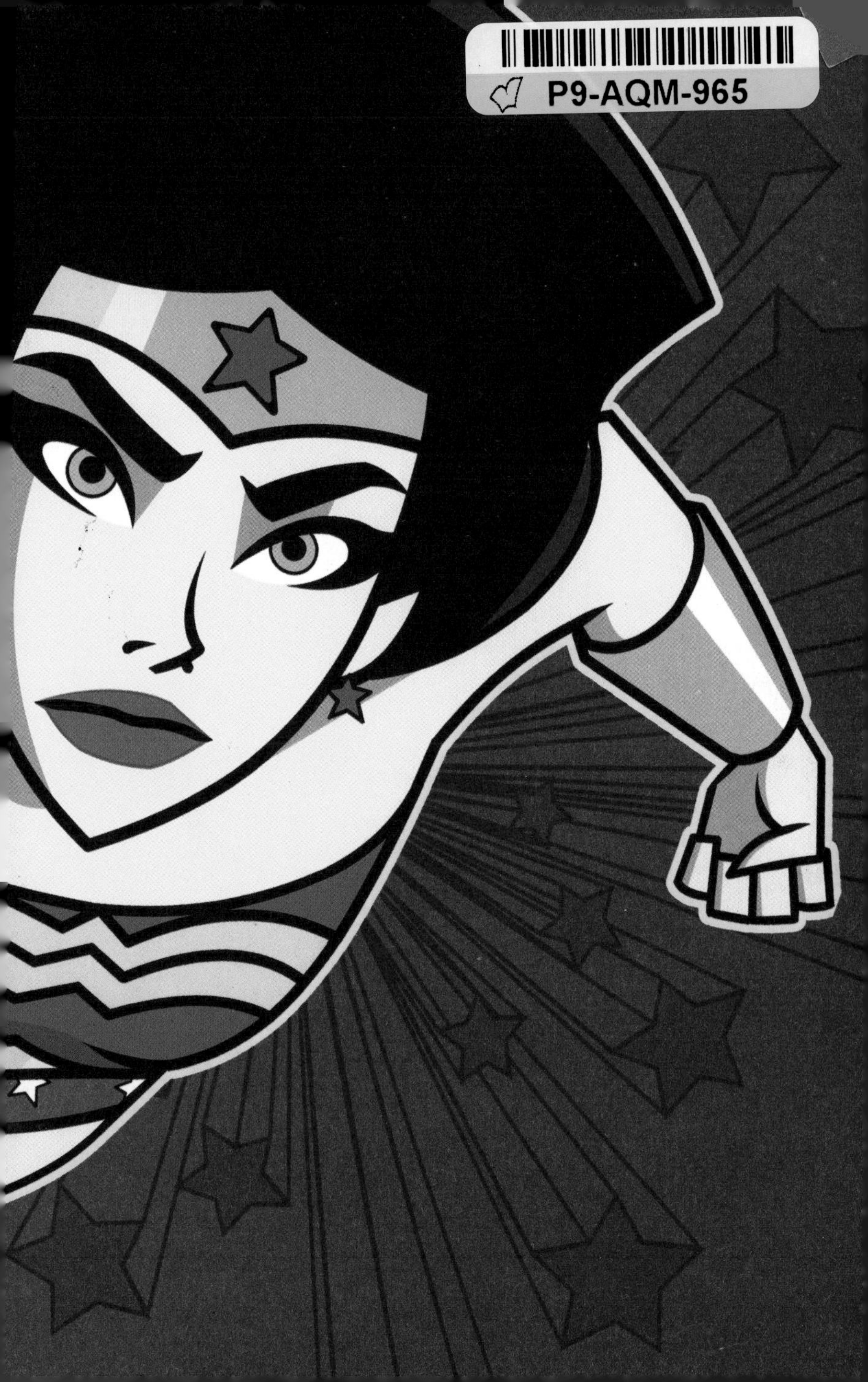

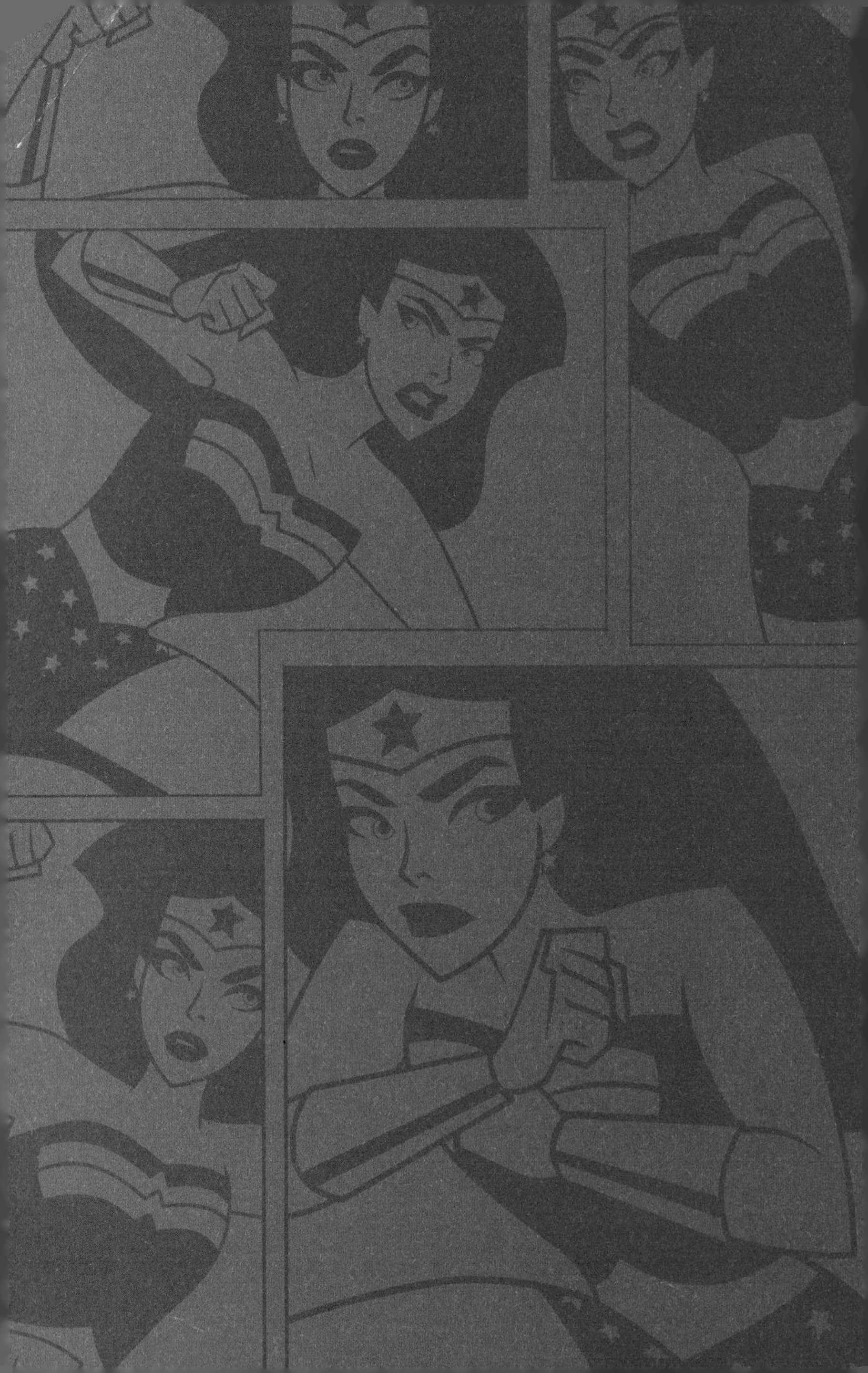

Wonder Woman

Attack of the Cheetah

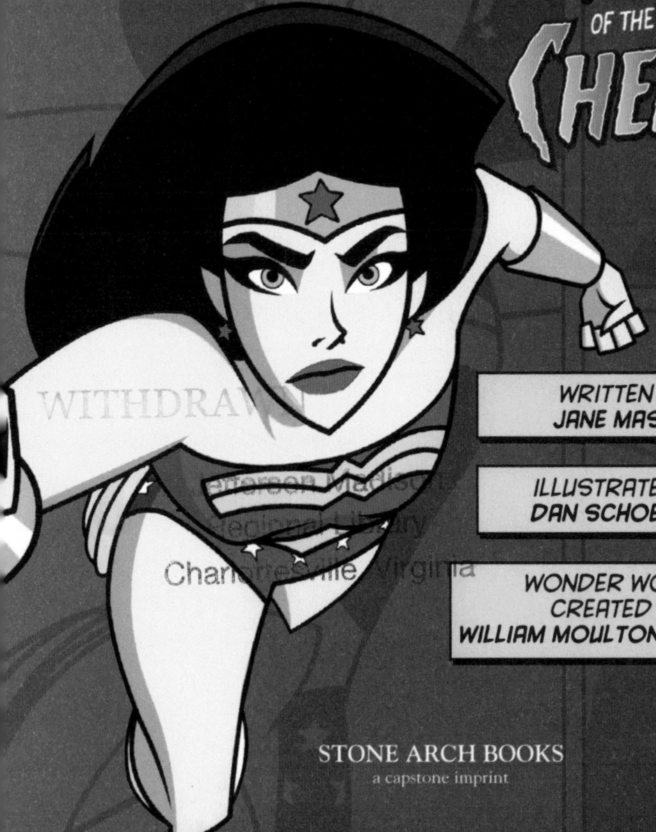

WRITTEN BY
JANE MASON

ILLUSTRATED BY
DAN SCHOENING

WONDER WOMAN
CREATED BY
WILLIAM MOULTON MARSTON

STONE ARCH BOOKS
a capstone imprint

Published by Stone Arch Books in 2010
A Capstone Imprint
151 Good Counsel Drive, P.O. Box 669
Mankato, Minnesota 56002
www.capstonepub.com

Library of Congress Cataloging-in-Publication Data

Mason, Jane B.
  Attack of the cheetah / by Jane B. Mason ; illustrated by Dan Schoening.
    p. cm. -- (DC super heroes. Wonder Woman)
  ISBN 978-1-4342-1886-5 (library binding) -- ISBN 978-1-4342-2254-1 (pbk.)
  [1. Superheroes--Fiction. 2. Cheetah--Fiction.] I. Schoening, Dan ill. II.
Title.
  PZ7.M4116At 2010
  [Fic]--dc22   2009029328

Summary: When a cheetah exhibit opens at the National Zoo in Washington,
D.C., Princess Diana arrives to witness the event. At the grand opening, the
rare cats suddenly escape, fleeing through a crowd of frightened zoogoers!
Diana quickly transforms into her secret identity, Wonder Woman, captures
the cats, and saves the day. But when the cheetahs continue their odd
behavior, only one thing can explain it. The cat-like super-villain, Cheetah, is
on the loose!

Art Director: Bob Lentz
Designer: Emily Harris
Production Specialist: Michelle Biedscheid

Printed in the United States of America in Stevens Point, Wisconsin.
092009
005619WZS10

TABLE OF CONTENTS

CHAPTER 1

SPECIAL DELIVERY

Princess Diana of Themyscira smiled. A crane was lowering a giant wooden crate into a grassy habitat. This was not your typical delivery.

For one thing, the words "live animals" were painted in large letters across the side of the crate. For another, low growls were coming from inside. The National Zoo had been waiting a long time for this package to arrive.

John Frank, Zoo Director, watched the crate get closer and closer to the ground.

"I can't believe they are finally here!" John said. The director stood inside a brand new exhibit called the Cheetah Hut. Judith Meyer, the head animal care specialist, stood next to him.

Princess Diana was there as well. She had been invited to attend the important event. "Believe it, John. They're here at last!" she said. She peered at the crate through the hut's glass window.

Judith flipped a switch. They could now hear what was happening on the other side of the glass. A zookeeper stepped forward and carefully pried open the crate. Then he quickly ran into a small shed inside the habitat.

At first, nothing happened. Then, suddenly, a flash of tan fur and black spots sprang out.

ROOAAARRR!! The cheetah let loose a deep growl. Then the large, lanky cat arched her back and leaped onto a large boulder.

"That must be Risa, the female," Judith said. "And judging from her behavior, she's definitely upset."

ROOAAARRR!! An answering growl came from inside the crate. A moment later, a pair of cheetahs leaped from the crate in unison. They landed together in a patch of grass. They stood back-to-back, nervous about their new home.

The cheetahs were beautiful, tall, and lean. Their golden fur was spotted with black. They had been delivered to the zoo by the CSP — Cheetah Survival Plan. The organization was helping to repopulate the species.

Diana watched the wild animals carefully. She admired their long, slender bodies. The three cats were siblings — two males and a female. All three were less than a year old. The males were bigger. But Risa, the female, seemed to be the leader.

Risa slowly circled on the large rock. She was daring anyone to challenge her. Orion and Nash, her brothers, crouched in the grass and twitched their tails.

"The drugs must have worn off already," Judith said, sounding a little alarmed. "I had hoped they would still be a little groggy when they arrived."

"It's all right," Diana said calmly. She reached for the handle of the door that led into the enclosure.

"I don't think it's safe —" Judith began.

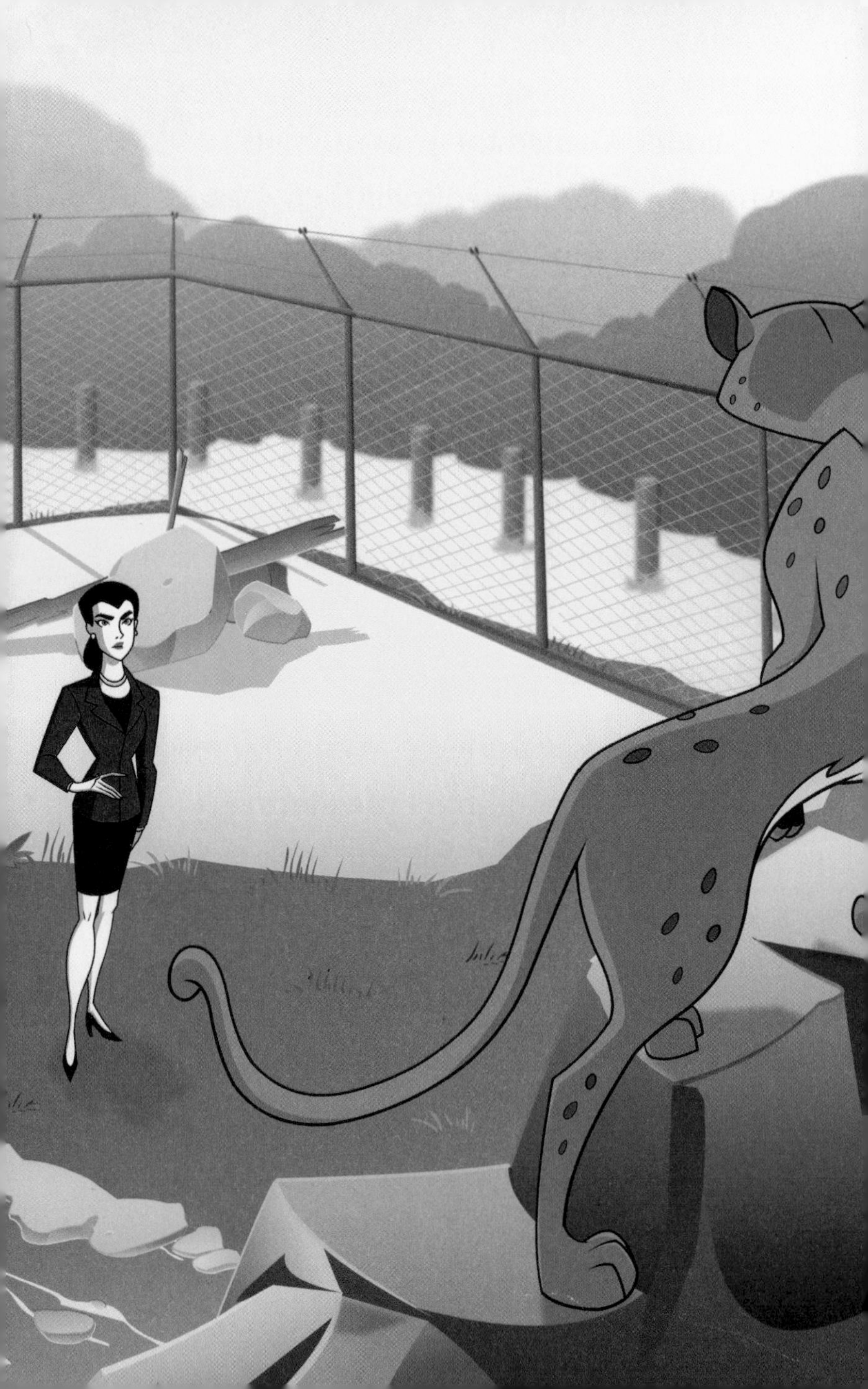

Princess Diana ignored the warning and stepped into the sunshine. Risa instantly swung her head to look at her. She laid her ears back and made a nervous growl.

Diana stood perfectly still, feeling the sun warm her back. "The sun must feel wonderful to you," she told the cat. "I'm sure your journey was long and difficult. But you are safe now. Everything is okay. We are going to take care of you."

Risa and Princess Diana locked eyes. Diana could tell that the cat was still afraid. Her tail darted back and forth with quick movements. On the other hand, her back was no longer arched. Her brothers were more relaxed, too. Orion and Nash were stretching in the tall grass.

Slowly, Diana moved closer. She kept eye contact with Risa.

Diana knew that the animal understood what she said. Diana had a special power when it came to communicating with animals. But there was only one way of knowing for sure if Risa trusted her.

Risa was crouching and ready to spring. If Princess Diana was going to retreat, now was her chance.

She didn't.

"I just want to make sure you're all right," Diana whispered. "Then, if you want me to, I will leave you alone."

Princess Diana slowly reached a hand out to Risa. The cat sniffed it for a minute. Then, Risa leaned in slowly, allowing Diana to scratch her ear.

Princess Diana beamed. "Who's a beautiful girl?" she said.

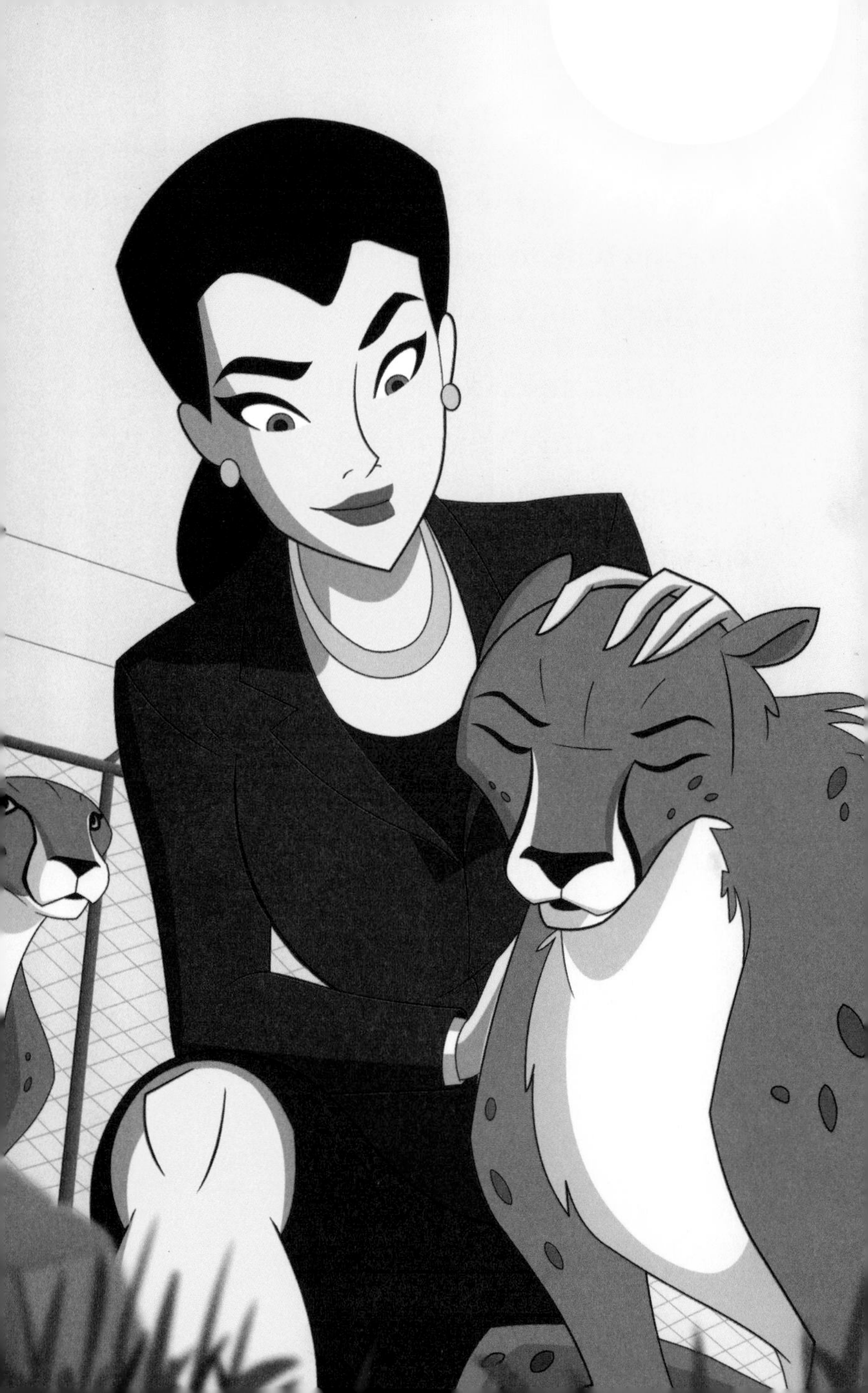

Orion lazily got to his feet. He made his way over, nuzzling Diana's hand. Nash, not wanting to be left out, curled around her legs like a house cat.

Judith came out of the hut. She walked slowly toward Diana and the cats. "That's incredible!" Judith said. "It's like they've known you since they were cubs."

Princess Diana gazed into Risa's eyes. Orion and Nash purred. Then they stretched out next to their sister in the sun. "I guess you could say I have a way with animals," she replied.

CHAPTER 2

FEEDING FRENZY

The next day, Diana smiled at the crowds as she entered the zoo gates. For the first time in months, the park was crowded. The people were here to see the newest addition to the zoo — the young cheetahs.

Princess Diana made her way through the crowds. Then she slipped inside the Cheetah Hut.

"Good morning," Judith said. "You're just in time for lunch." She was holding a bucket of raw meat for the cats. Another bucket was on the floor next to her feet.

"I was hoping I was on time," Princess Diana said. She loved to be there when the cats were fed. After eating, they would stretch out in the sun and groom each other. It was wonderful to see them happy in their new home.

Judith went outside to herd the cats into their indoor space. Since they were almost fully grown, it was safest to contain them while the food was being laid out. Wild cats often acted in unpredictable ways when they were around food.

"We're all set," Judith called as she closed the latch on the door. **CLANK!**

Diana picked up the extra bucket of food and walked into the enclosure. She and Judith split up. They each set the meat out on various rocks and logs for the cheetahs to find.

Afterward, Diana and Judith returned to the hut to watch the cheetahs eat.

As Risa stepped into the sunshine, Diana felt uneasy. Something was wrong. Risa looked the same as the day before, but different. She seemed nervous as she approached a hunk of meat, as if she felt someone was going to swoop in and steal it. Then, with a pounce, Risa tore into the beef. CHOMP!

"I guess she was hungry," Judith said, laughing nervously.

CHOMP! CHOMP! Behind Risa, Orion and Nash were devouring their meals. They ate in giant gulps, looking around warily.

While the cats were eating, Judith stepped outside. She was going to refill their water trough, just like she did every day.

Today, though, was different. Diana felt the tension in the air as Nash stopped eating. He watched Judith with narrowed eyes. Then, in a flash, the big cat leaped toward her!

Princess Diana didn't hesitate. She began to spin, creating a tornado of amazing speed. **FLASH!** In a moment, her civilian clothes disappeared. Flashes of blue, red, and gold glowed in the hut. By the time she came to a stop, Diana was gone — Wonder Woman had arrived!

Wonder Woman threw open the door just as Nash pounced on Judith. **THUD!**

"Nash, stop!" Wonder Woman called in a calm voice. She knew the cat could understand her. However, he did not acknowledge her presence, or her words, at all.

Orion noticed her, but not in the way she had hoped. He sprang off the rock. Then he charged right at her!

Wonder Woman reached her arms out. She caught the cat by its paws in midair. She held him over her head with ease. Wonder Woman carried the cat to the indoor space. Then she gently tossed him inside.

Behind her, the growls were fierce. Judith was rolling around on the ground with Nash. "Help!" she cried out.

Wonder Woman reached for her Golden Lasso. She swung it above her head, flicking her wrist with each twirl. She sent the lasso flying after three spins. WHOOOOSH! It flew through the air, catching Orion around the neck. With an easy jerk of her arm, Wonder Woman pulled the cat off the zookeeper.

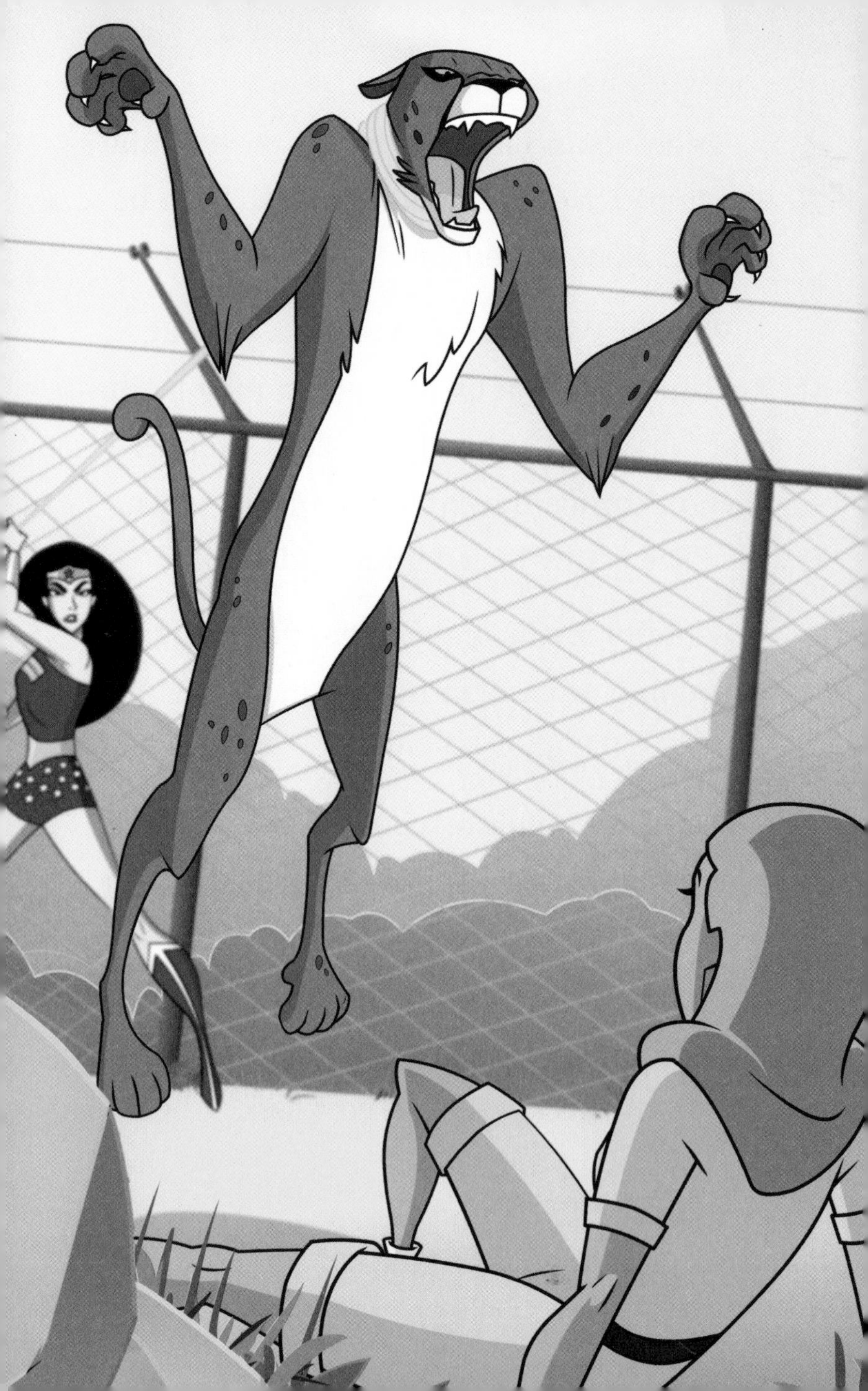

Orion hissed and snarled. He fought hard as Wonder Woman forced him into his enclosure with his brother.

"Risa!" Judith called, pointing.

Just as Wonder Woman turned around, the female cheetah leaped off a high rock. Risa sailed over the exhibit fence. She landed gracefully on her four paws. Zoo visitors screamed. **AAAAAHHH!**

Wonder Woman sprang into the air. She propelled herself over the fence. **THUD!** She landed hard on her red boots, right next to a young zoo visitor.

"Cool!" he said. He watched her speed off after the cheetah.

Wonder Woman ran through the crowds. She could see Risa straight ahead, a blur of gold. Suddenly, the cat made a sharp turn.

As Wonder Woman rounded the corner, she saw Risa leap onto the roof of a café.

Risa, stop! Wonder Woman said in her mind. *Be calm, my friend.* The cheetah did not listen to her.

Wonder Woman barely slowed down before she jumped. The roof was covered in gravel, and she skidded to a halt. The cat was about to jump into the crowded food court below.

"There it is!" someone shouted, pointing at the rooftop.

The cat hesitated for a split second. It was just enough time for Wonder Woman to tackle it. *WHAM!*

The cat hissed and swiped hard at Wonder Woman. Its powerful paw struck her magic bracers. *KRAK!*

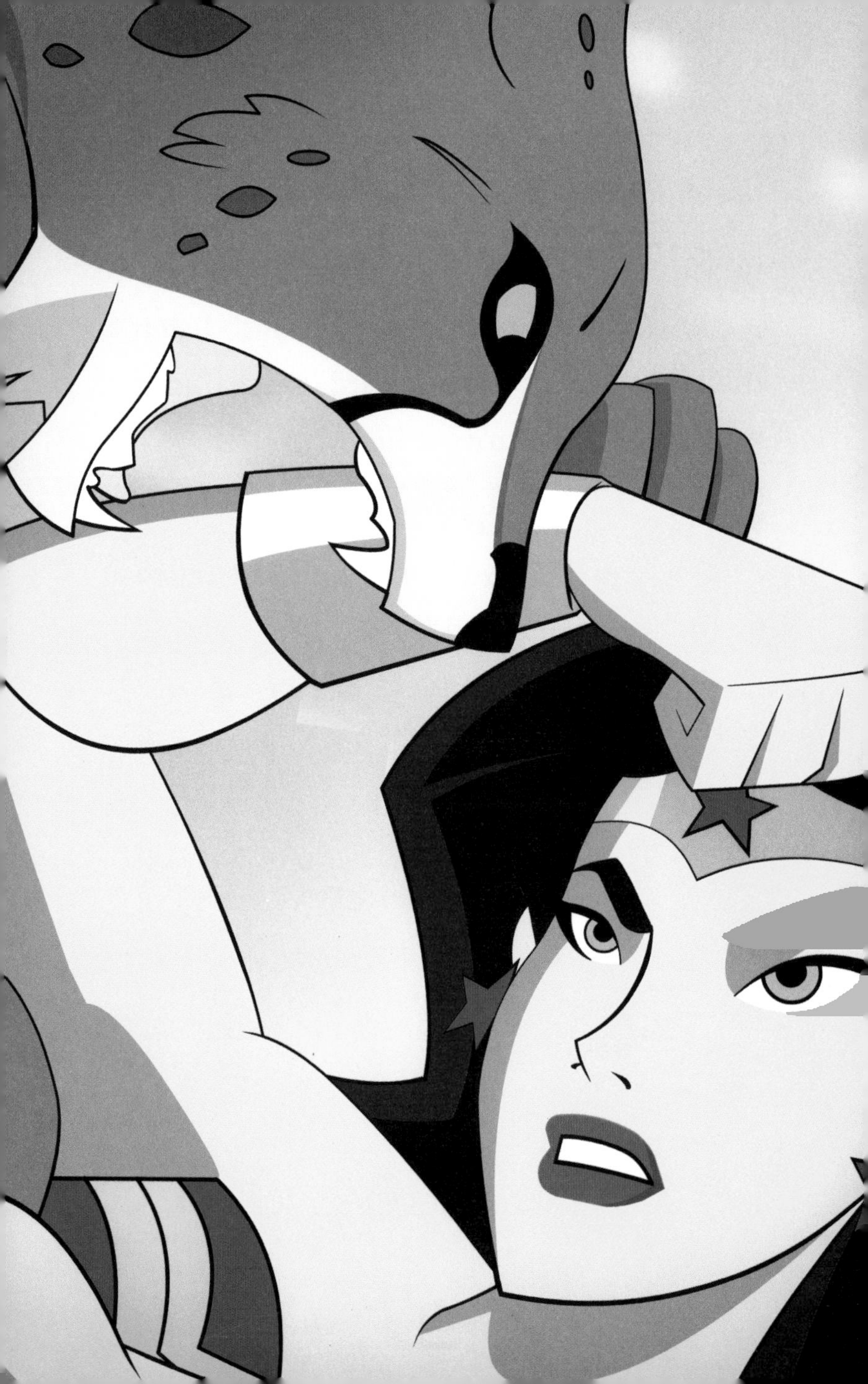

She tried to call out to the cat once more. *It's me, Risa!* she silently told the cheetah. *I'm not going to hurt you.*

Risa paused for a second as if to listen, then hissed and swiped hard. Once again, Wonder Woman raised her arm up to deflect the blow. **THWACK!**

Quickly, Wonder Woman grabbed Risa by the legs. She lifted the cat and swung it over her bare shoulders. She began to carry the angry animal back to its proper habitat.

AN *ALARMING* DISCOVERY

That night, Diana sat alone in her apartment. She felt uneasy. The cheetahs had been safely returned to their exhibit, but Diana had been unable to calm them. It was as if the cats had forgotten that they had been her friends.

Sighing, Diana picked up the TV remote. **CLICK!** As soon as the screen came to life, she gasped. The first thing she saw was Nash pouncing on Judith. Then it flashed to Wonder Woman lassoing Orion. Then it showed Risa's amazing leap to freedom.

Close-ups of hundreds of screaming zoo visitors filled the TV screen. Nobody had been hurt. Even Judith was completely unharmed, but the TV news reporter didn't mention any of that.

"Public safety is extremely important to the zoo," Director John Frank told the reporter. "We are doing everything we can to make sure something like this never happens again."

Princess Diana's heart went out to the Zoo Director. The National Zoo had worked long and hard to get those cheetahs, and now they were causing problems. City officials did not take aggressive animals lightly.

And they shouldn't, Diana thought. *Aggressive animals are dangerous.*

The cheetahs' behavior was highly strange. The cats had been adapting very well until that day. Something went wrong.

The TV screen cut back to the cheetah chase. Wonder Woman was racing after Risa. As the big cat rounded the corner, Wonder Woman noticed something on the television screen. Something she hadn't noticed during the chase.

It made Diana's blood run cold.

Diana hit pause. Standing in the crowd of screaming, panicked people was a shadowy figure. It was a lean, graceful-looking woman with fiery red hair. She stood perfectly still. Her eyes were pinched at the corners. Her smile was wicked.

It was Wonder Woman's archenemy — the super-villainess, Cheetah!

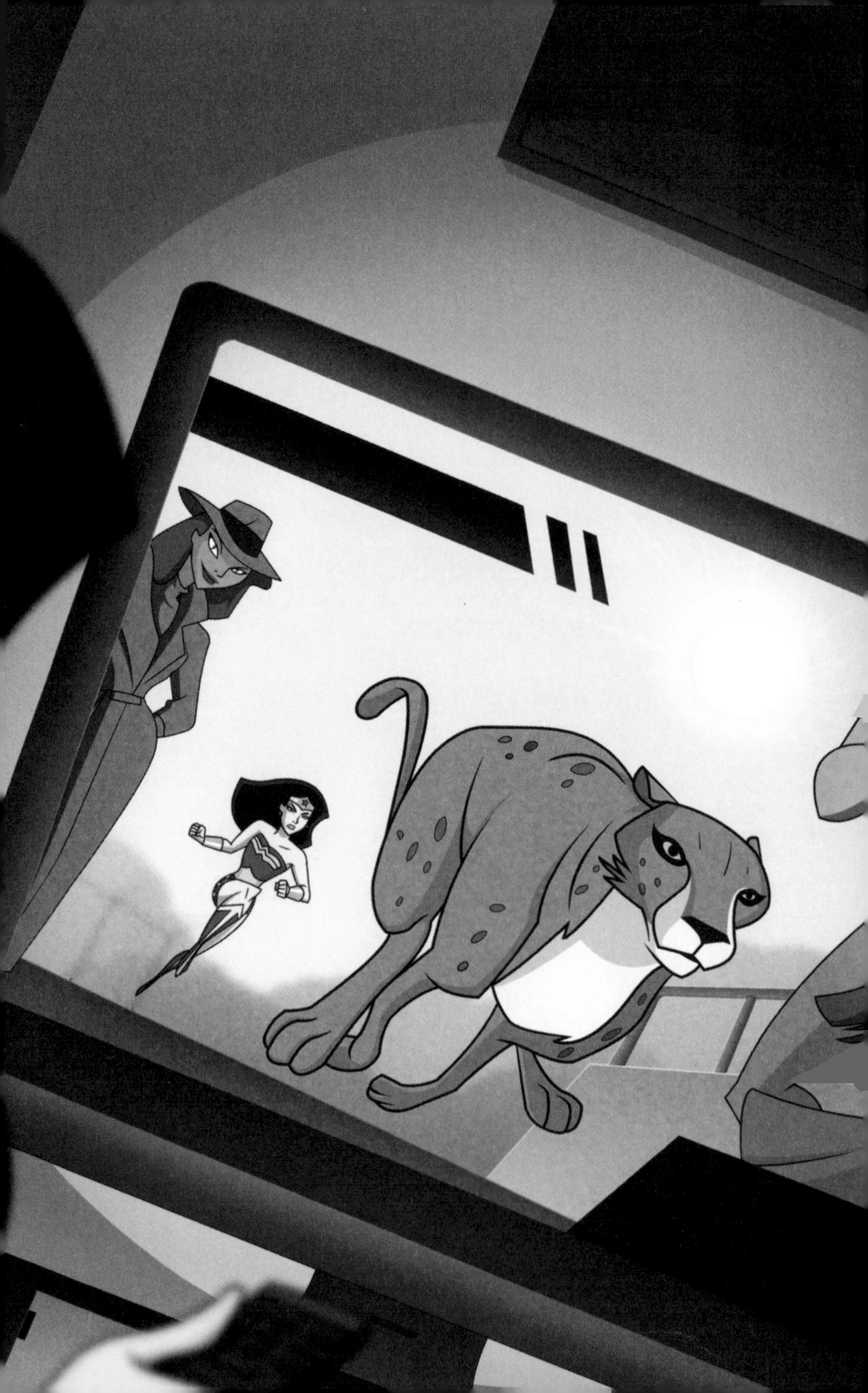

CHAPTER 4

POUNCED

The next morning, Princess Diana sat at her kitchen table. She was eating breakfast and sipping her tea. The daily newspaper sat nearby. The front page read: CHEETAHS RUN WILD AT LOCAL ZOO. WONDER WOMAN SAVES THE DAY.

Diana stared down at the headline. She couldn't stop thinking about how she had spotted her nemesis, Cheetah, on the TV screen the night before. She knew that more trouble was coming. But what was Cheetah planning this time?

The phone rang. Diana picked it up.

"Princess Diana? It's John Frank," said a serious voice over the phone. "I have good news and bad news."

Princess Diana was not sure what she wanted to hear first. "Give me the bad news," she told the Zoo Director.

"City officials are breathing down my neck," John said. "If another attack occurs, they're going to shut down the zoo."

"But the cheetahs didn't really attack," Princess Diana insisted. "It's more like they were —"

"Scared, I know," said John. "Judith said the same thing. Thanks to Wonder Woman, no one was hurt. But the public saw a trio of animals that looked wild. So that's what they're going to focus on."

Diana sighed. This *was* bad news. "So what's the good news?" she asked.

"The good news is that KRVP Television News is coming this morning. They want to do a report on the cheetahs. We need to show the people that the cheetahs are peaceful. Then the crowds will keep coming. I'm calling to ask if you can be here. You have such a way with the cats."

Diana bit her lower lip. *I did, before Cheetah showed up,* she thought. There was no doubt that the evildoer was responsible for the cheetahs' wild behavior.

"I'll be there, John," Princess Diana promised. "You can count on me."

CLICK! Diana hung up the phone. She hurried to get dressed. The sooner ⌐ the zoo, the better.

Princess Diana left through the door of her apartment. Suddenly, Cheetah landed right in front of her!

"Well, what do we have here?" she purred. "If it isn't Miss Goody Two-Shoes."

Diana whirled and twirled, transforming into Wonder Woman. "I don't mean to be rude, but I can't chat," she said. "I'm afraid I've got somewhere else to be."

"It won't help," Cheetah said. She darted into Wonder Woman's path. The feline villain moved with amazing speed. "These are three animals you can't control."

Wonder Woman was confused, but didn't show it. One thing she knew about Cheetah is she liked to hear herself talk. If ___ kept quiet, the proud Cheetah would ___ some part of her plan.

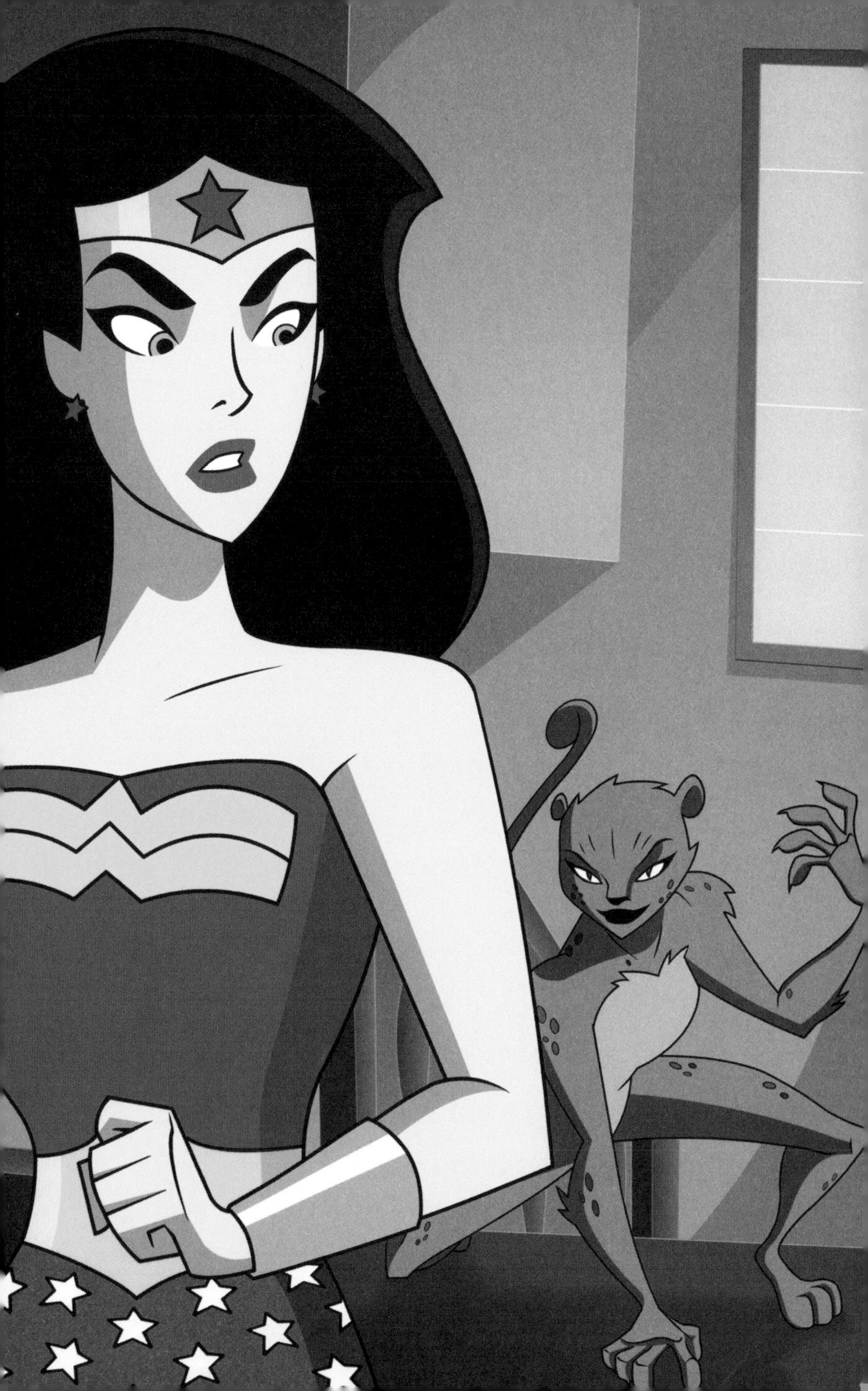

"Really?" Wonder Woman said, trying to get her enemy to continue.

Cheetah arched her feline back. "Of course," she said. "You didn't think I'd stand by and let you cage such beautiful wild animals, did you?" Her laugh echoed in the air. "No, no, I couldn't have that. So I decided to ruin your pet project." Her face twisted into a sneer. "I must say my scheme worked out even better than I thought. Now all I have to do is keep you away from my little kitties."

"*Your* kitties?" Wonder Woman asked.

"Yes, *my* kitties," Cheetah admitted. "How else could I control them? It was so easy, really. Last night, I just waited until midnight. Then I led *your* cheetahs to an open area outside the zoo."

"They're safe there now," Cheetah said. "Such fierce, beautiful creatures simply cannot be caged!"

Wonder Woman felt a flash of worry for the real Risa and her brothers. Cheetah may have been trying to help the animals, but they were probably confused and upset. Diana also felt foolish. She had known for some time that her nemesis had recently acquired a trio of cheetahs. They were unlike the zoo's cheetahs in every way. And they were under her complete control.

With the secret out, Wonder Woman was even more anxious to get to the zoo. That meant getting past the speedy Cheetah, which was no easy task. There was no time left to waste. *WHOOOOSH!*

In a blur of blue and red, Wonder Woman burst away at super-speed!

Wonder Woman soared into flight.

Cheetah was ready and waiting. Below, in her cat form, Cheetah raced down the street. She leaped over cars and trucks. "You won't escape me this time!" Cheetah howled.

As Wonder Woman flew toward the zoo, Cheetah leaped onto a city bus. While the passengers screamed, Cheetah prepared to pounce. "Just a little lower now . . ." she murmured to herself.

Wonder Woman dipped down to avoid a road sign. It gave Cheetah her chance. Her long back arched as she flew through the air toward Diana.

KRASSSHHH! The two women collided together on the pavement outside the zoo gates.

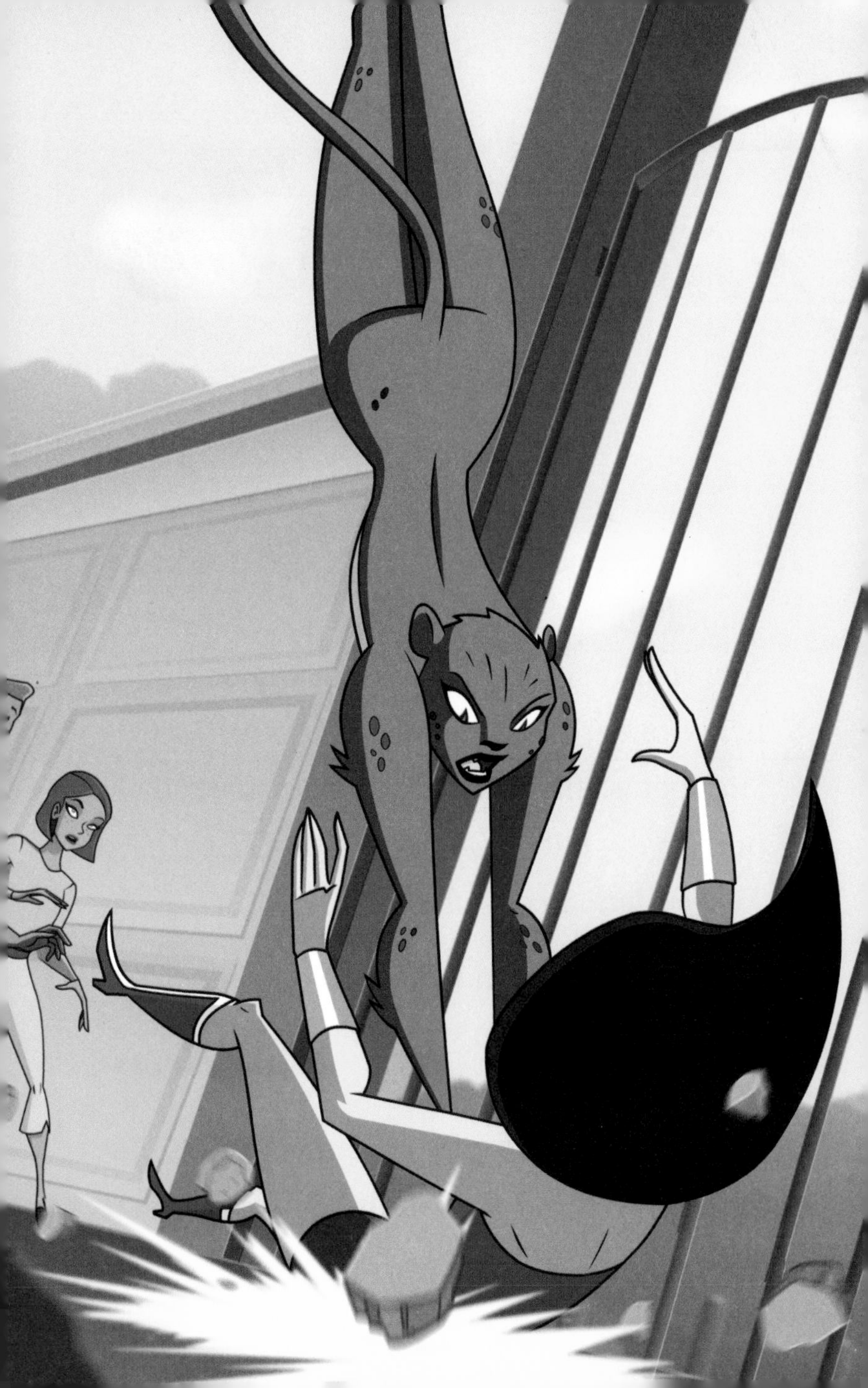

CHAPTER 5

LIVE AT THE NATIONAL ZOO

With Wonder Woman stunned, Cheetah leaped off her prey. Then she raced into the zoo. Her long tail flicked excitedly behind her. Wonder Woman got back to her feet. She spotted the KRVP News truck parked next to the gates. *Oh no!* she thought. *The TV crew has already arrived!*

Wonder Woman leaped to her feet. She sprinted into the zoo at super-speed. Her red boots pounded on the paved path. By the time she got to the cheetah exhibit, the television crew had already set up.

John Frank was standing next to Nancy Nosall, the head reporter for KRVP News. He looked extremely nervous.

Inside the exhibit, Judith looked even more nervous. She stood far away from the cheetahs. Her arms were crossed over her chest defensively.

Things did not look good. Wonder Woman wanted to stop the interview before one of the impostor cheetahs caused real harm.

"Three . . . two . . . one," called the cameraman loudly. "We're rolling!"

"Hello, viewers, I'm Nancy Nosall. Today I'm reporting live from the National Zoo. We're at the Cheetah Hut, the new home of a trio of happy cats," Nancy spoke into the camera.

The camera panned past Nancy into the habitat. Judith was slowly approaching a cheetah in a field of grass within the enclosure. The cheetah was lounging in the sun on a large flat rock. It looked bored.

"The woman with the cheetahs is Judith Meyer. She heads up the cheetah program here at the National Zoo. They are trying to repopulate this endangered species," Nancy told the camera.

Half-hidden behind a tree, Wonder Woman watched Orion carefully. She was ready to spring into action if her help was needed.

She could see that Orion wasn't actually Orion at all. However, the remarkably similar-looking cheetah seemed calm enough, for now.

Suddenly, a snarl erupted from deep in the cheetah's throat. **ROOAAARRR!!**

Orion's impostor got to his feet and crouched. In less than an instant, he had pounced on top of Judith!

In the blink of an eye, Wonder Woman leaped over the fence. She pulled the cheetah off the caretaker. Then, she wrestled the cat into the enclosed pen.

Before Wonder Woman could get the door closed — **WHAM!** — the other two cheetahs were on her. They became a mass of red and blue and gold. They rolled from one side of the habitat to the other.

POW! A cheetah's sharp claws dug into Wonder Woman's arm. Outside of the enclosure, the reporter and crowd cringed and gasped.

The fight seemed to go on and on. Wonder Woman was working hard to control and tire out the beasts.

All at once, Wonder Woman twisted with blinding speed. She untangled herself from the cheetahs. Then she stood quickly and grabbed one by its tail.

The animal cried out in surprise, but Wonder Woman was gentle. She did not hurt him.

She easily lifted one wild cat over her head. Then Wonder Woman grabbed the other exhausted animal around the waist. With one cheetah in each arm, she carefully carried them to the indoor enclosure. Their captive sister was waiting for them inside.

"Noooo!" came a shriek from afar.

Wonder Woman had been kept busy fighting off the impostor cats. She had completely forgotten about the plan's evil mastermind — Cheetah herself!

A red-haired female stood on a nearby roof. She sprang into the air, turning into a powerful cheetah. Then she soared at breathtaking speed toward her target.

Fractions of a second later, the dangerous super-villain pounced squarely on Wonder Woman's shoulders. The blow sent her flying forward through the air.

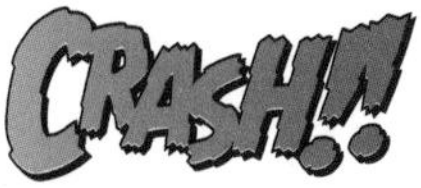
CRASH!!
Wonder Woman smashed into the enclosure's concrete wall. Cheetah rolled forward, flipping herself back onto her feet. Then she turned toward her foe.

"How dare you interfere with my plans!" Cheetah said, letting loose a mighty roar.

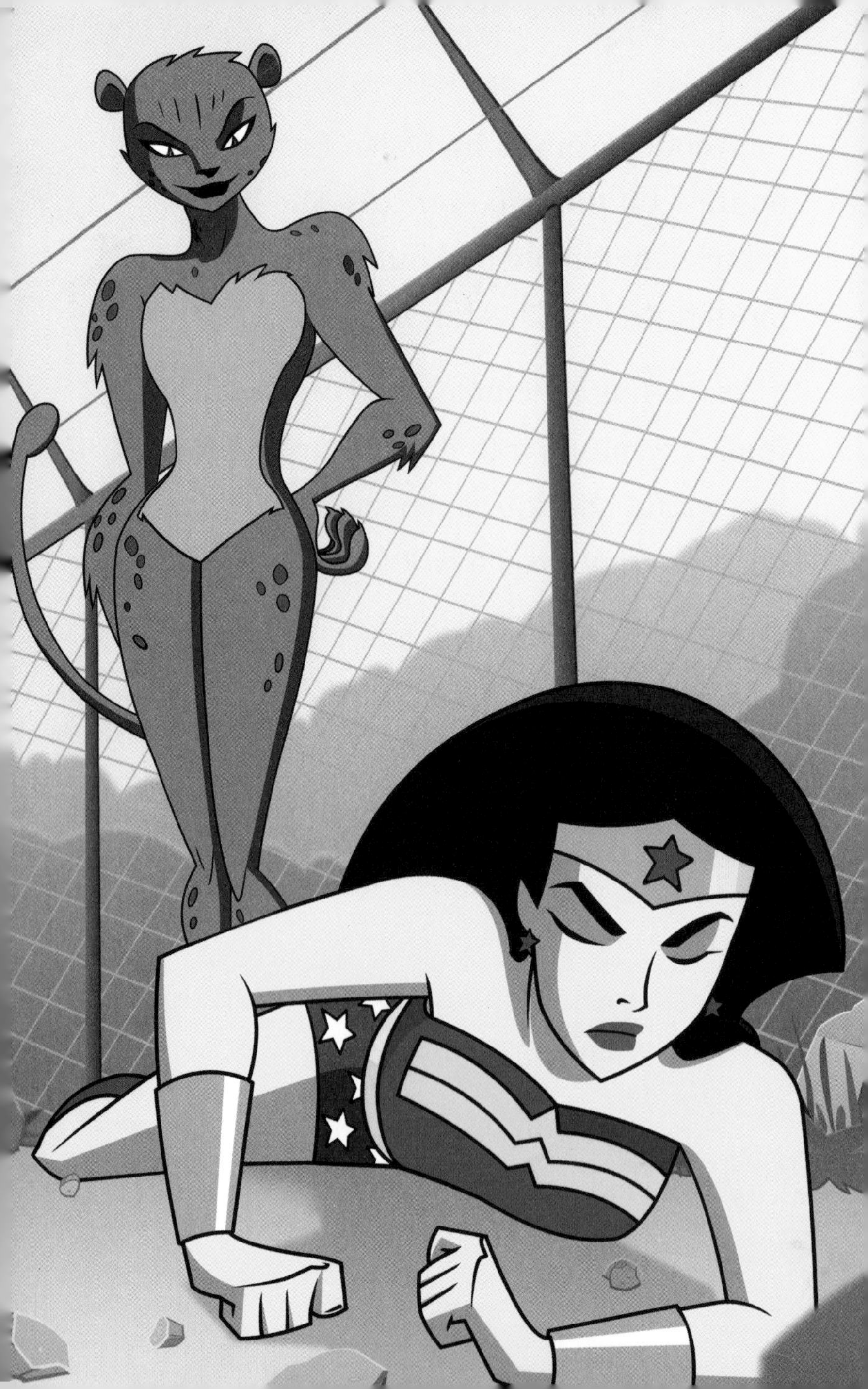

The fallen Wonder Woman lifted her head to meet Cheetah's gaze. Wonder Woman climbed back to her feet and dusted herself off. She continued to stare straight into Cheetah's angry feline eyes.

"We're protecting them from danger by giving them a safe place to live here in the zoo," Wonder Woman argued. "The cheetah species' numbers are dwindling, and they are near extinction. We're just trying to save them."

"Save them?" Cheetah challenged. "What do the world's fastest animals need protection from?!"

Cheetah lurched forward with super-speed, paws swinging. But Wonder Woman was ready for the attack. She easily deflected both paw swipes with her bracelets. CHING! CLANK!

Wonder Woman grabbed Cheetah's paws and braced herself. With the super-villain stuck in her grasp, she knew she would be a captive audience.

"Adult cheetahs are fast, that much is true," Wonder Woman agreed. "But the younger cheetahs aren't. They are easy prey for their predators."

Wonder Woman tightened her grip on Cheetah's arms to drive home her final point. "Since their numbers are so small now, their species isn't as strong as it used to be," Wonder Woman said, flexing and forcing Cheetah to her knees.

Cheetah let out a howl of pain. Wonder Woman loosened her grip. She didn't want to hurt her opponent.

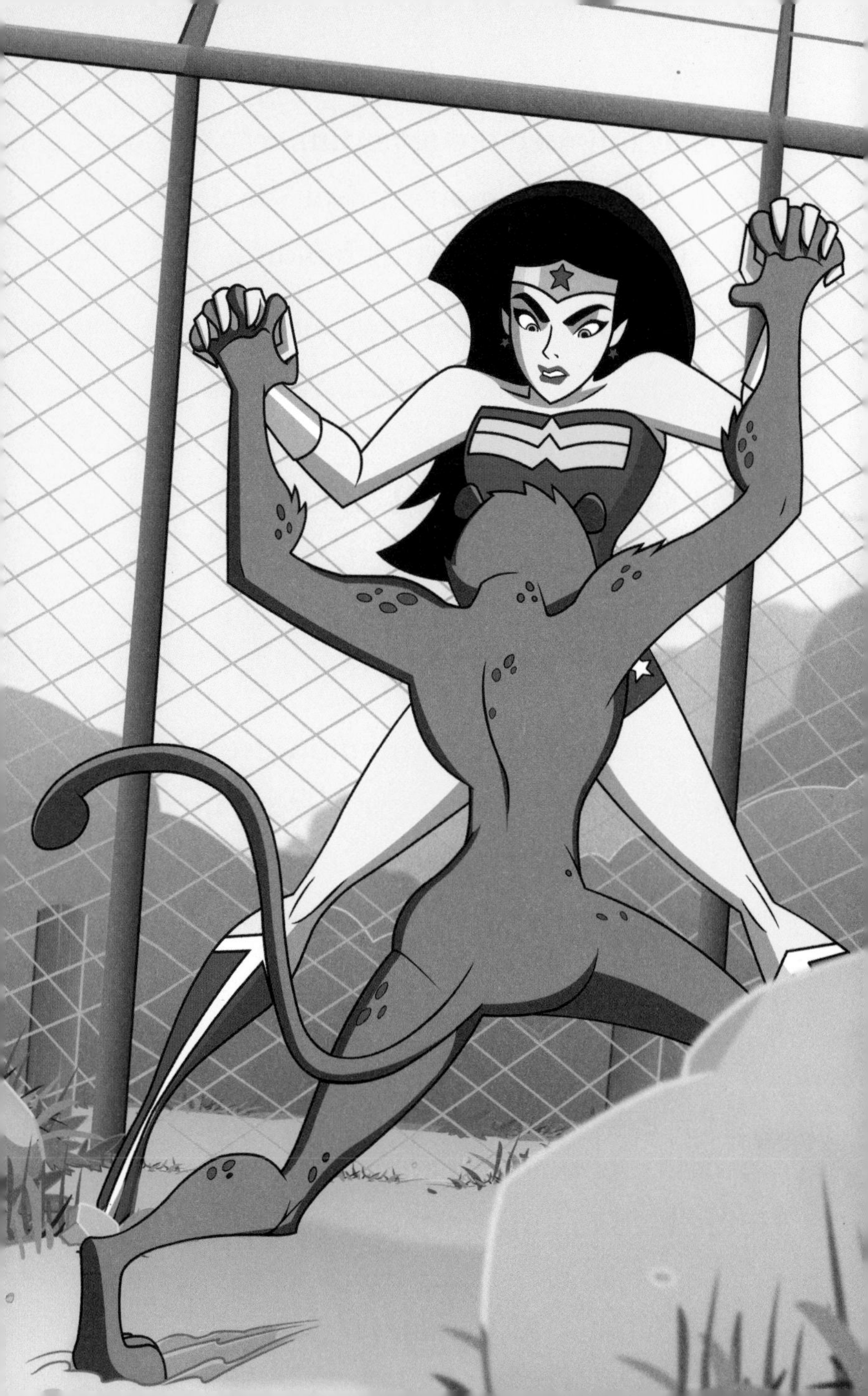

Cheetah used the opportunity to slip free from Wonder Woman's grasp! She dashed off to the roof of a nearby building.

Cheetah landed on the roof above. Swinging her arms upward, Wonder Woman flew up to the base of the building. Wonder Woman paused and freed her Golden Lasso from her belt. She twirled it three times. Then she let it fly — just as Cheetah leaped from the building.

The lasso wrapped around Cheetah's legs in midair. The cat came crashing down to the ground. Wrapped in the Golden Lasso's noose, she was powerless.

The normally graceful villain had fallen right in front of the TV News camera. Wonder Woman walked over to her defeated opponent. "Sometimes cats need a little help to land on their feet," she said.

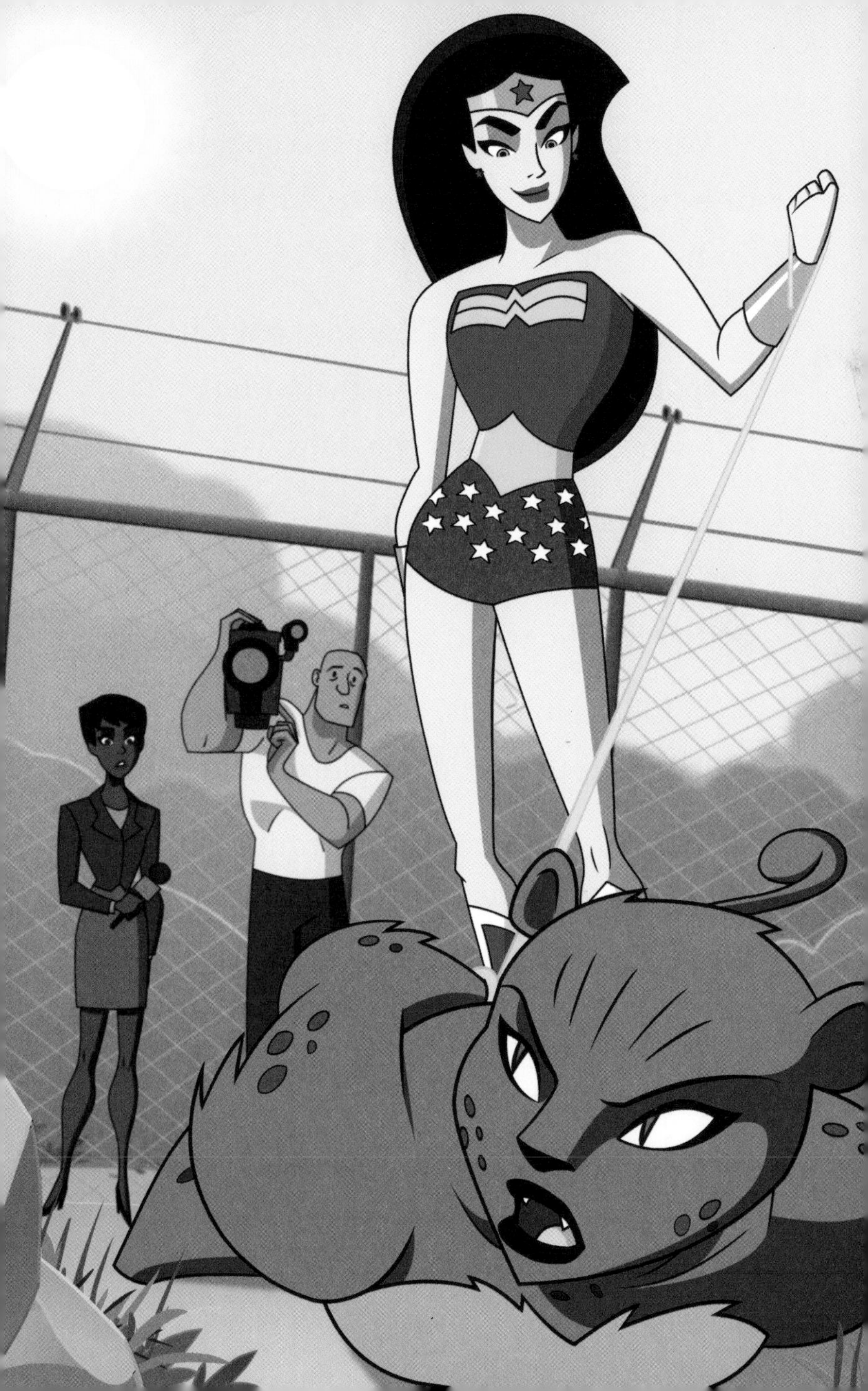

Wonder Woman set her red boot on Cheetah's back. Then she a placed a hand on her own hip.

"Please, Cheetah," she said politely. "Explain to the people just what has happened to our new cheetahs."

Wrapped up tightly in Wonder Woman's Lasso of Truth, Cheetah had no choice. She had to tell the world what she had done.

"I hid them away, and put my own trained cheetahs in their place," she purred.

The crowd gasped. John Frank stepped forward. "Where are they?" he asked.

Wonder Woman put a hand on John's shoulder. "They are safe, John," she assured him. "Cheetah might be a villain, but she would never hurt another cat."

Cheetah glared up at Wonder Woman.

"She's right," Cheetah hissed. "Your cheetahs are perfectly safe."

* * *

That night, Diana and John Frank celebrated with Judith at a cozy restaurant.

"It's too bad you missed it," John told Diana. "It was quite a show! I don't think it was what KRVP News was expecting. Even Nancy Nosall was speechless!"

Judith laughed, and her eyes lit up. "Wonder Woman was amazing," she said. "She caught those cheetahs like they were harmless little kittens!"

"Thanks to her, the National Zoo is going to survive after all," John agreed.

Diana nodded and smiled. "Yes," she said, raising a glass in a toast. "Wonder Woman has saved the day once again."

INVISIBLE PLANE
SECRET FILES

FILE NO. 3758 >>> CHEETAH

ENEMY)) ALLY FRIEND

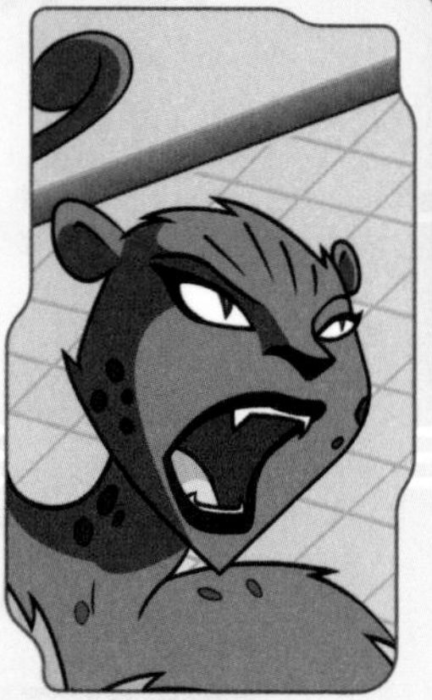

REAL NAME: Barbara Ann Minerva

OCCUPATION: Biologist

HEIGHT: 5 ft 9 in **WEIGHT:** 120 lbs

EYES: Brown **HAIR:** Auburn

POWERS/ABILITIES: Superhuman strength, speed, and agility. Her claws and teeth are razor sharp, capable of slicing through stone.

BIOGRAPHY

Dr. Barbara Ann Minerva was a successful biologist who was working on ground-breaking genetics research. Her tests, however, were very expensive. She ran out of money to fund them. Desperate to finish her studies, Dr. Minerva tested her highly experimental research on herself. As a result, her body was transformed into a half-human, half-cheetah hybrid. Shunned by the scientific community, and seen as a freak by the rest of the world, Cheetah has turned to crime to fund her efforts to once again become human.

MISSION

CAPTURE THE CAT:

Cheetah is Wonder Woman's most cunning and clever enemy. Her cat-like agility and super-strength make her a formidable fighter, too. To make matters worse, Cheetah is prone to animal-like rages at any given time.

In order to overcome such a dangerous foe, Wonder Woman must formulate a plan of attack in order to capture the cat!

WEAPON

LASSO OF TRUTH:

Wonder Woman's Lasso of Truth is capable of snaring Cheetah, weakening her super-speed and super-strength. More importantly, the lasso would also force her to speak nothing but the truth while wrapped in its unbreakable golden coils. In the capable hands of Wonder Woman, the lasso can get to the root of Cheetah's trickery, so she can stop Cheetah in her tracks.

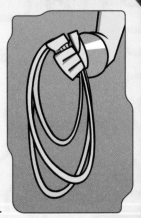

BIOGRAPHIES

Jane Mason is no super hero, but having three kids sometimes makes her wish she had superpowers. Jane has written children's books for more than fifteen years and hopes to continue doing so for fifty more. She makes her home in Oakland, California, with her husband, three children, their dog, and a gecko. Her boys are begging for a pet cheetah, but Jane is holding firm.

Dan Schoening was born in Victoria, B.C. Canada. From an early age, Dan has had a passion for animation and comic books. Currently, Dan does freelance work in the animation and game industry and spends a lot of time with his lovely little daughter, Paige.

GLOSSARY

enclosure (en-KLOH-zhur)—an area closed in by a fence or walls

habitat (HAB-uh-tat)—the place and natural conditions in which a plant or an animal lives

impostor (im-POSS-tur)—someone who pretends to be something that he or she is not

lanky (LANG-kee)—very tall and thin

nemesis (NEM-uh-sis)—a fierce opponent or rival

scheme (SKEEM)—a plan or plot to do something that is evil or dishonest

tension (TEN-shuhn)—a feeling of worry, nervousness, or suspense

unison (YOO-nuh-suhn)—to do something as one, or together

warily (WAIR-uhl-ee)—in a watchful or guarded manner

DISCUSSION QUESTIONS

1. Do you think zoos are a good place for endangered animals? Why or why not?

2. If Wonder Woman didn't have superpowers, would she still be a hero? What makes her a hero — her abilities, or her character? Explain.

3. This book contains ten illustrations. Which one is your favorite? Why?

WRITING PROMPTS

1. Cheetah is a shape-shifter. If you could transform into any animal, what would it be? What powers would your animal form give you? Write about your adventures as a shape-shifter.

2. Wonder Woman's Golden Lasso forces anyone within its grasp to speak only the truth. If you could make anyone tell you anything, would you use that ability? Why or why not? If so, what would you want to know, and who would you ask?

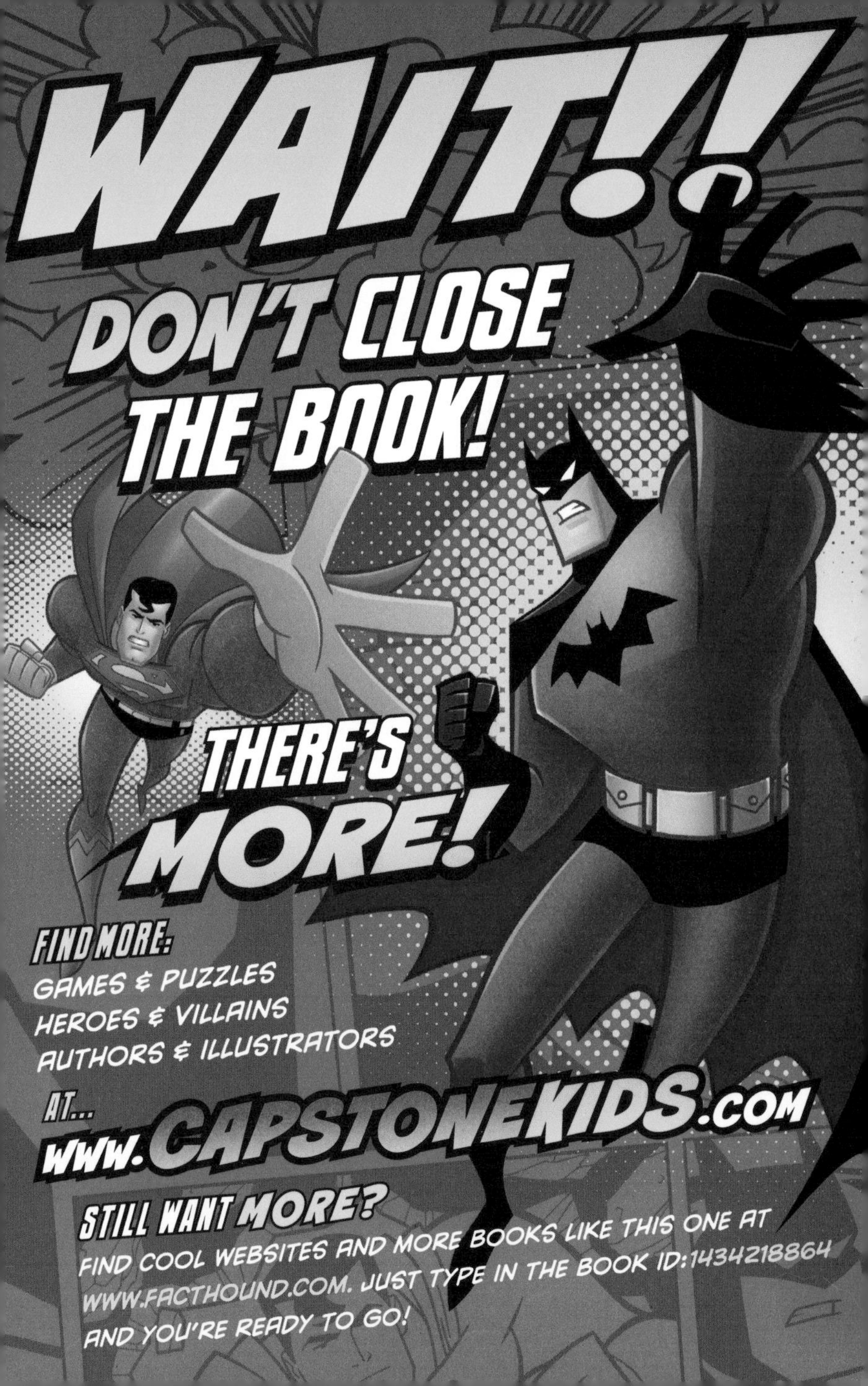
WAIT!!
DON'T CLOSE THE BOOK!
THERE'S MORE!
FIND MORE:
GAMES & PUZZLES
HEROES & VILLAINS
AUTHORS & ILLUSTRATORS
AT...
WWW.CAPSTONEKIDS.COM
STILL WANT MORE?
FIND COOL WEBSITES AND MORE BOOKS LIKE THIS ONE AT WWW.FACTHOUND.COM. JUST TYPE IN THE BOOK ID:1434218864 AND YOU'RE READY TO GO!

MORE NEW WONDER WOMAN ADVENTURES!

SUPER DC HEROES
WONDER WOMAN
CREATURE OF CHAOS
ADVENTURE

CREATURE OF CHAOS

SUPER DC HEROES
WONDER WOMAN
TRIAL OF THE AMAZONS
DAHL · SCHOENING
ADVENTURE

TRIAL OF THE AMAZONS

SUPER DC HEROES
WONDER WOMAN
SIMONSON
SCHOENING
MONSTER MAGIC
ADVENTURE

MONSTER MAGIC

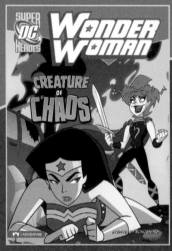

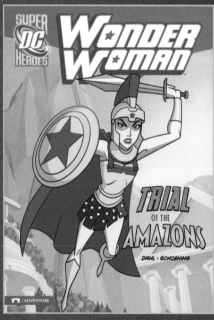

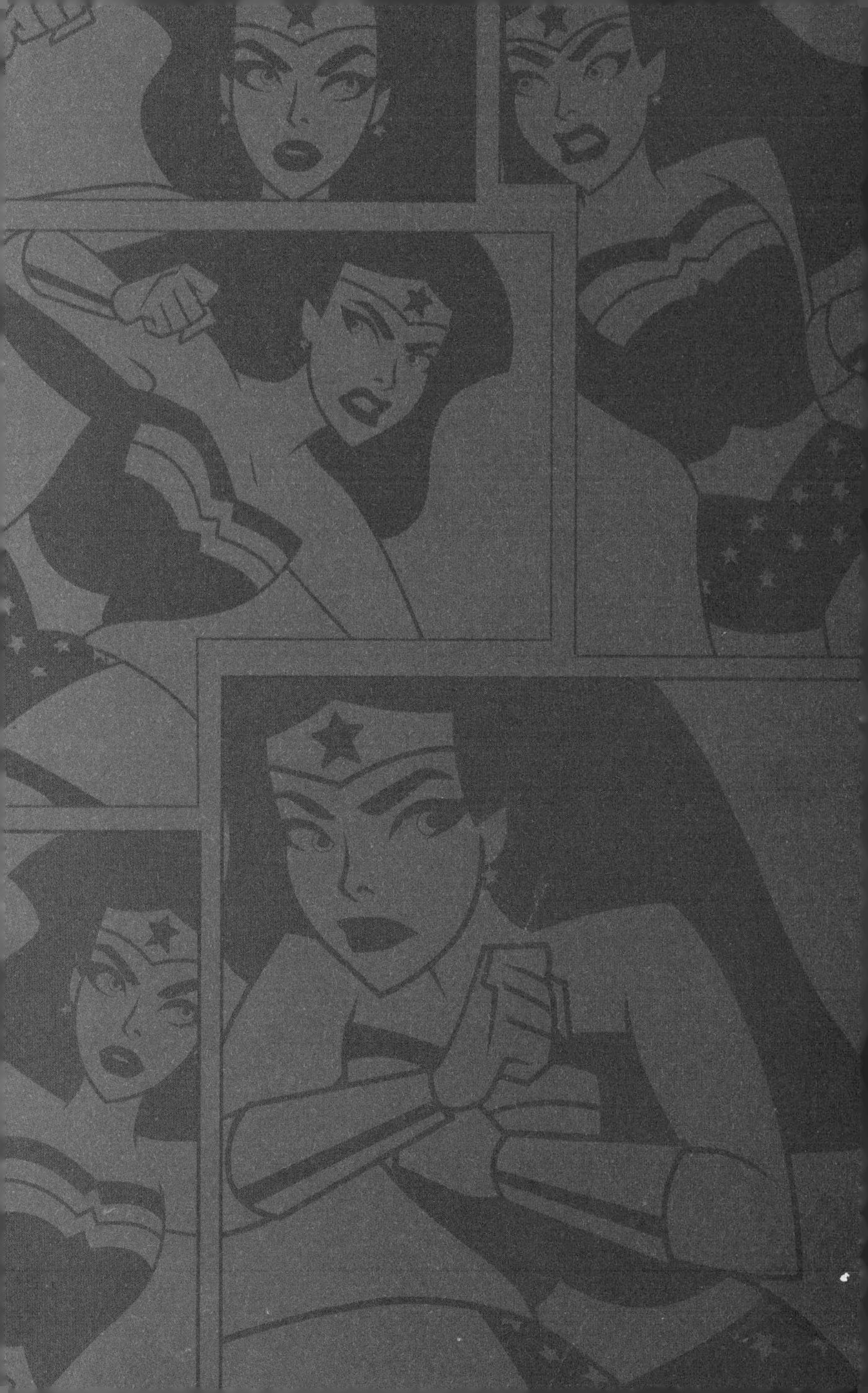

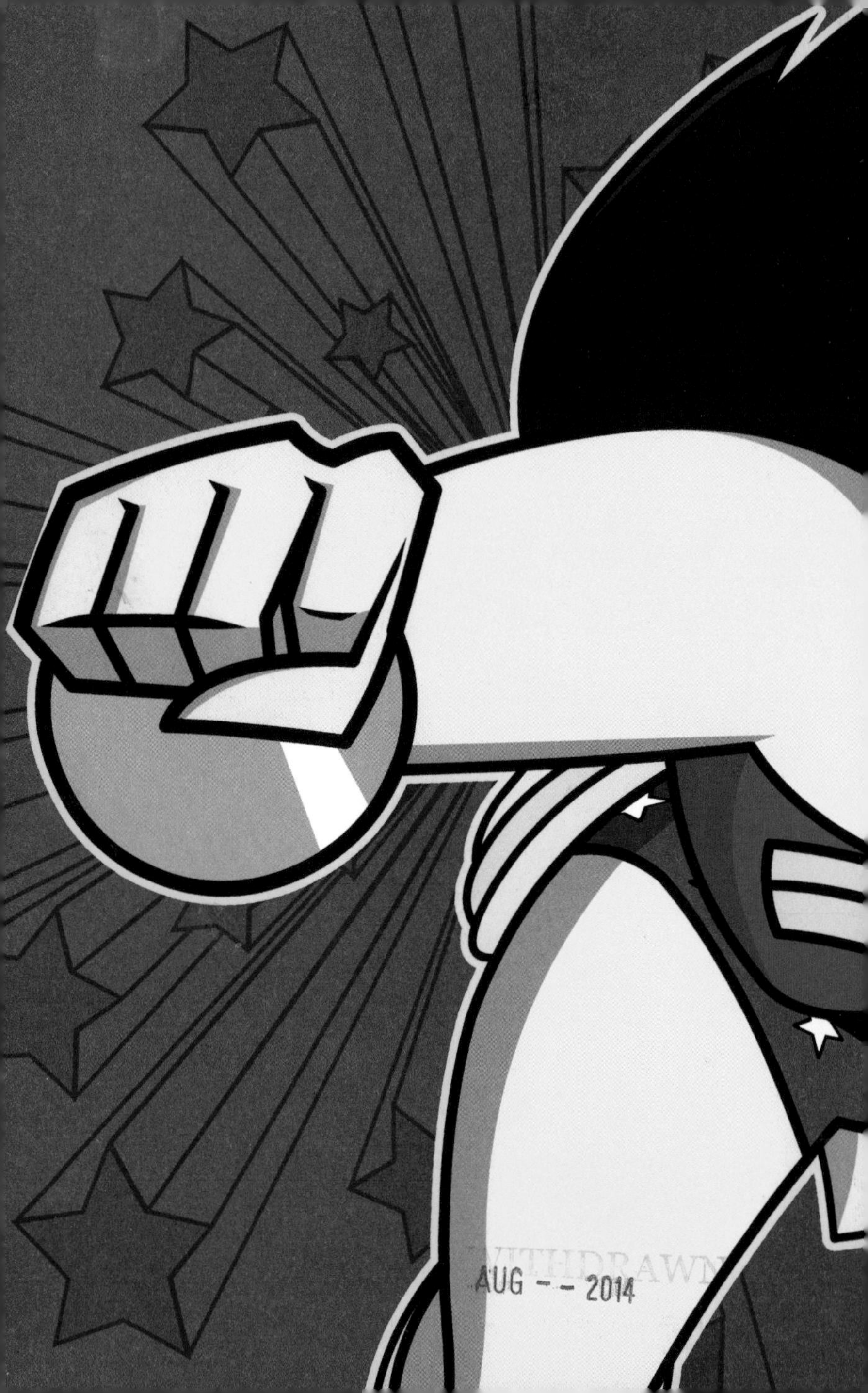